MERCER MAYER'S

CRITTERS OF THE NIGHT®

ROAST AND TOAST

What time is it? It's time for the midnight barbecue! What do you eat at a midnight barbecue? Why, roasted hot dogs on toasted buns, of course. And the fun is only just beginning!

Children will be able to read this book all by themselves—because it's written in simple language especially for beginning readers.

This book comes from the home of
THE CAT IN THE HAT
Beginner Books
A DIVISION OF RANDOM HOUSE, INC.

For a list of some other Beginner Books, see the back endpaper.

Wanda   Jack   Thistle   Axel

Bones

Snake

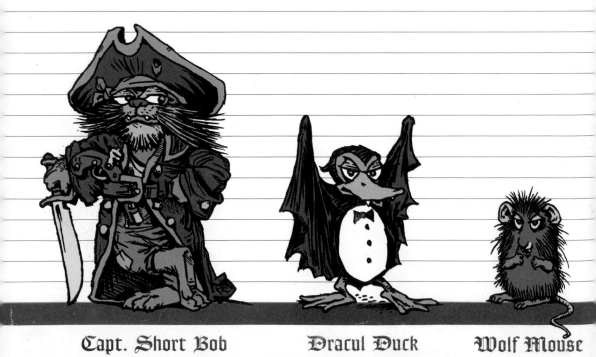

Capt. Short Bob   Dracul Duck   Wolf Mouse

Groad   Frankengator   Moose Mummy

Uncle Mole   Zombie Mombie   Auntie Bell

http://www.randomhouse.com/

Library of Congress Cataloging-in-Publication Data

Farber, Erica.
Roast and Toast / written by Erica Farber and J. R. Sansevere.
p.   cm. — (Mercer Mayer's Critters of the night)
"Beginner Books."
SUMMARY: Creatures enjoy food and fun on the beach at Midnight Bay.
ISBN 0-679-87376-7 (trade). — ISBN 0-679-97376-1 (lib. bdg.)
[1. Beaches—Fiction. 2. Animals—Fiction. 3. Stories in rhyme.]
I. Sansevere, John R. II. Title. III. Series: Critters of the night.
PZ8.3.F21667Ro 1998 [E]—dc21 97-31628

Printed in the United States of America   10 9 8 7 6 5 4 3 2 1

 A BIG TUNA TRADING COMPANY, LLC/J. R. SANSEVERE BOOK

BEGINNER BOOKS is a registered trademark of Random House, Inc.

MERCER MAYER'S

CRITTERS OF THE NIGHT ®

ROAST AND TOAST

Written by Erica Farber
and J. R. Sansevere

BEGINNER BOOKS®
A Division of Random House, Inc.
New York

My name is Fang.
I've come for you.
Come to the
midnight barbecue!

Quick, grab your cape.

Come on. Let's go.

There's lots to do.
It's fun, you know!

We fly and fly
into the night.

Zoom past the moon.

Then take a right.

Or was that a left?

Please check the map.

I am so tired.

I need a nap.

Let's go by plane.

Or take a car.
Midnight Bay
is very far!

Here comes my friend.

Let's wave hello.

A train can be
the way to go.

Another friend

is on a bike.

A bike is fun.

I like to bike.

We land on sand.

We meet and greet.
Then after that,
it's time to eat!

But first we cook.

You toast the buns.

I roast the hot dogs.

This sure is fun!

Pickled eyeballs,
green slime, and chees[e]
are great on top.
Do try them, please!

Have two hot dogs.

Have three. Have four.

Have five. Have six.

You must have more!

When we are full,
it's time for fun.
We hop. We skip.

We jump.

We run.

Now it is time
to take a dip.

We belly-flop.

We do a flip.

We swim.

We surf.

We water-ski.
Uh-oh! That wave is
bigger than me!

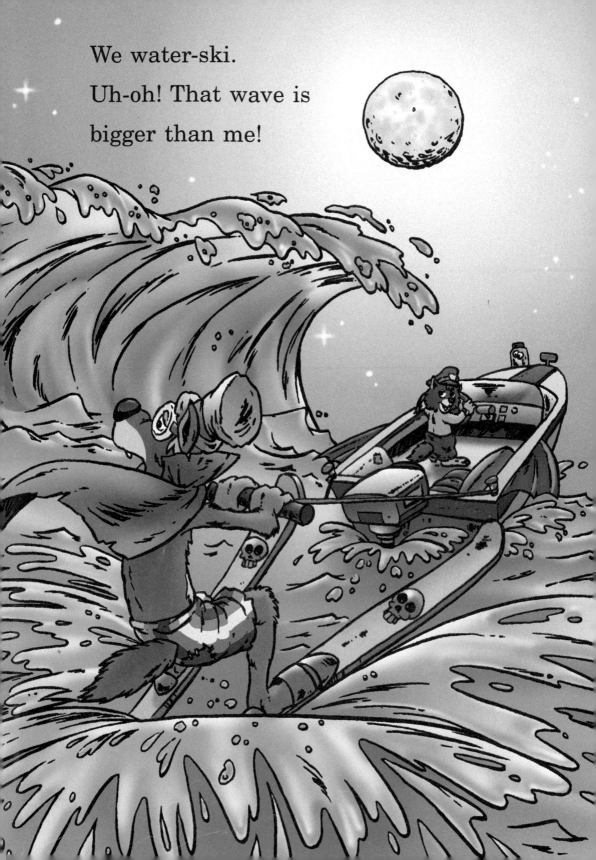

When we are done,
we play some ball.
Your team is short.
My team is tall.

We sit and fish,
but nothing bites.

We hunt
for crabs.

We fly
our kites.

A shell for you.
A pail for me.
We build a castle
by the sea.

Our friends all cheer.
Our castle's great.
Here comes a wave.

Uh-oh! Too late!

We build a fire.
We sing a song.
We pluck a harp.
We bang a gong.

The sky is pink.

We start to yawn.

It's time to go.

It's almost dawn.

The next full moon,
we hope that you
will come to the
midnight barbecue!

I CAN READ IT ALL BY MYSELF

Beginner Books

Have you read
these all-time favorite
Beginner Books?

THE BEAR DETECTIVES
by Stan and Jan Berenstain

THE CAT IN THE HAT
By Dr. Seuss

GO, DOG. GO!
by P. D. Eastman

GREEN EGGS AND HAM
by Dr. Seuss

IT'S NOT EASY BEING A BUNNY
by Marilyn Sadler

PUT ME IN THE ZOO
by Robert Lopshire

SPOOKY RIDDLES
by Marc Brown